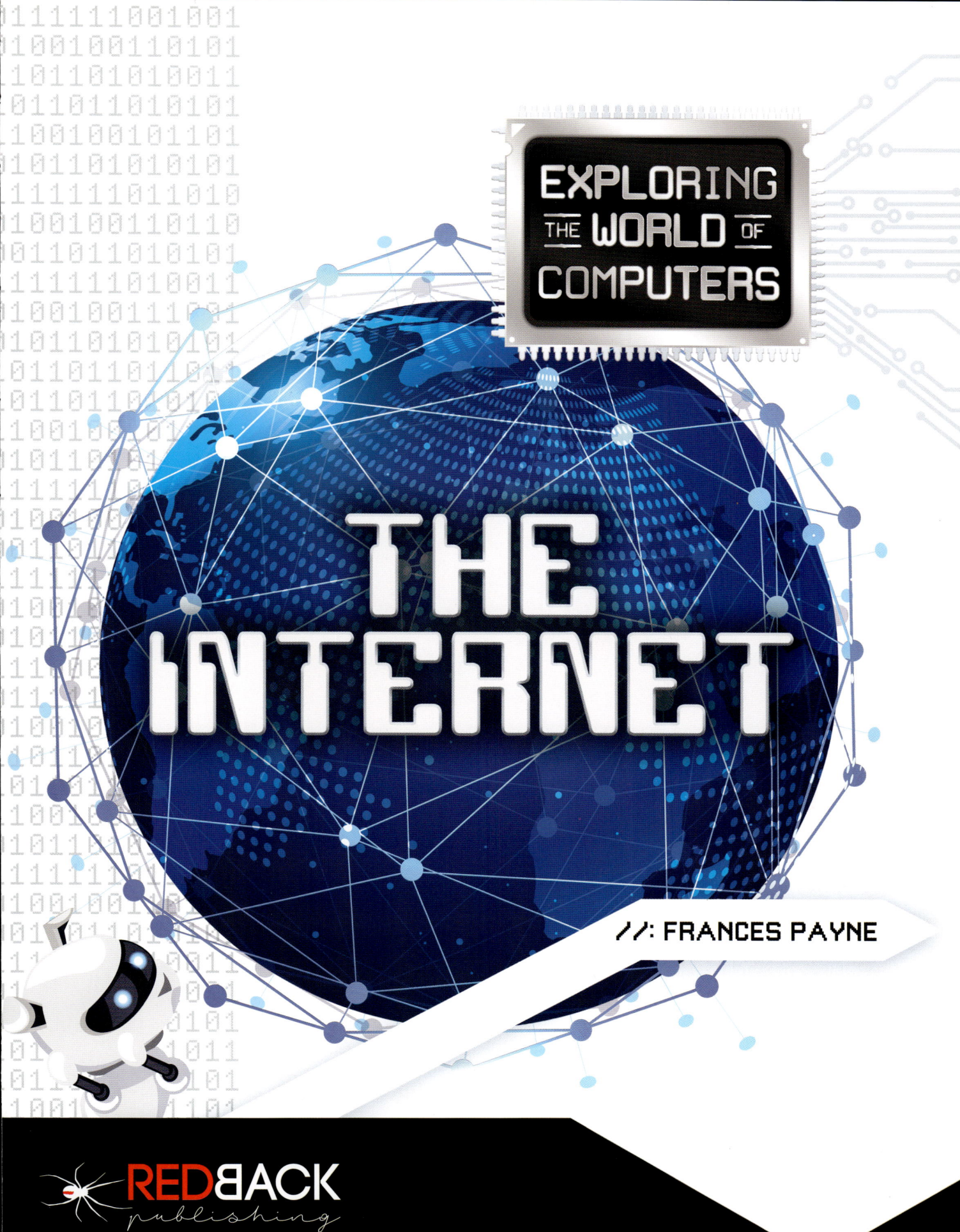

EXPLORING THE WORLD OF COMPUTERS

THE INTERNET

//: FRANCES PAYNE

REDBACK publishing

Redback Publishing
PO Box 357 Frenchs Forest NSW 2086
Australia

www.redbackpublishing.com
orders@redbackpublishing.com

ISBN 978-1-925860-71-9

Author: Frances Payne
Editor: Marianne Lindsell
Designer: Redback Publishing

Original illustrations © Redback Publishing 2020
Originated by Redback Publishing

Printed and bound in China

Acknowledgements
Abbreviations: l—left, r—right, b—bottom, t—top, c—
centre, m—middle
We would like to thank the following for permission to
reproduce photographs: (Images © shutterstock)
p14ml By STRINGER

FSC
www.fsc.org

MIX
Paper from
responsible sources
FSC® C020056

NATIONAL LIBRARY OF AUSTRALIA

A catalogue record for this
book is available from the
National Library of Australia

Contents

History of the Internet

The Internet is composed of millions of computers all around the world. They connect to each other allowing users to search the files stored on them. These files produce the webpages that we see on our computer screens when we do a search on an Internet browser.

Computers interact with each other via modems that connect through telephone lines, satellites or other services.

History of the Internet

The history of the Internet began in universities in the USA during the 1970s. People working there invented ways to send messages amongst themselves using their computers. In the 1990s, businesses were able to connect their computers as well and send messages to each other.

Before the Internet existed, long-distance communication depended on telephones, fax machines, two-way radios, telex machines, and sending letters and telegrams. Communication using the Internet has increased enormously since the 1990s, resulting in interactions that are faster and cheaper. As a result of the Internet, many people in remote regions of the world now have access to immediate and detailed information about what is happening in other countries, something that was once impossible for them.

10 Tips for Internet Safety

Do

1. Logout of a password protected site when you are finished using it. This stops someone else seeing what you have been doing online.
2. Keep your passwords private. Passwords should include letters and numbers, and they could even be phrases.
3. Look for the padlock symbol in the address bar at the top of the browser before doing any online buying.
4. Ignore 'friend requests' on social media from strangers.
5. Tell a trusted adult if you discover that someone is saying unpleasant things about you on social media.

Don't

1. Don't use the word PASSWORD as your password. It is too easy for someone else to guess.
2. Don't type in all your personal details just because a site asks for them. Think about why they want to know all about you.
3. Don't click on blinking links that promise free downloads. They may send viruses or malware to your computer.
4. Don't be an Internet troll who upsets other people by posting nasty comments.
5. Don't believe everything you see or read on the Internet. Fake news is everywhere!

DOWNLOAD A COPY OF THIS POSTER TO USE AT HOME OR AT SCHOOL

- Go to www.redbackpublishing.com
- Find the entry for this book and click on the link for the Internet Safety poster.

Who Owns Internet Content?

Copyright

Just as the content of books is owned by the people who write or publish them, Internet content is also owned by its creators. This ownership of creative content is called copyright. Although it is easy to copy words and images that someone has placed on a website, this does not mean that anyone else can reuse them, make profit from them or claim them as their own work.

The copyright owner statement often appears at the bottom of a webpage. The © symbol means that the creator of the page, its words or its images is claiming ownership of the content.

People who misuse copyrighted words or images are engaging in Internet piracy.

Creative Commons

Creative Commons is an international organisation that aims to allow copyright owners of creative material to make their work available for others to use through a licensing scheme. There are various levels of usage, varying from allowing complete freedom to copy and alter a work, to allowing only copying with no alterations permitted. A number of websites list content with Creative Commons licenses.

Creative Commons licenses may allow children and schools to use licensed work they find on the Internet, without breaking copyright laws. The user needs to acknowledge the person who first wrote the words or produced the image.

Search Engines

Search engines are software that searches for webpages in the World Wide Web. The most popular search engines are Google, Yahoo and Bing. Search engines use algorithms or instructions that find webpages based on words entered into the online search box by the computer user.

SEO (Search Engine Optimisation)

SEO, or Search Engine Optimisation, is a way of improving a website by including certain words and other content that make a webpage rank higher amongst the search engine results when someone does an online search. SEO is a growing business worldwide and it is likely to provide many opportunities for employment in the future.

What is the Dark Web?

The Dark Web includes parts of the Internet that are not searchable in the usual way. The people who create these webpages do not want everyone else to read or see what they contain. They do this by using encryption which turns their webpages into codes that search engines cannot read. Criminals and people who want to hide their communications use the Dark Web. Because of this, use of the Dark Web will attract the attention of law enforcement authorities.

Web Browsers

Web browsers are a type of software that allows computer users to find webpages.

Popular Web Browsers

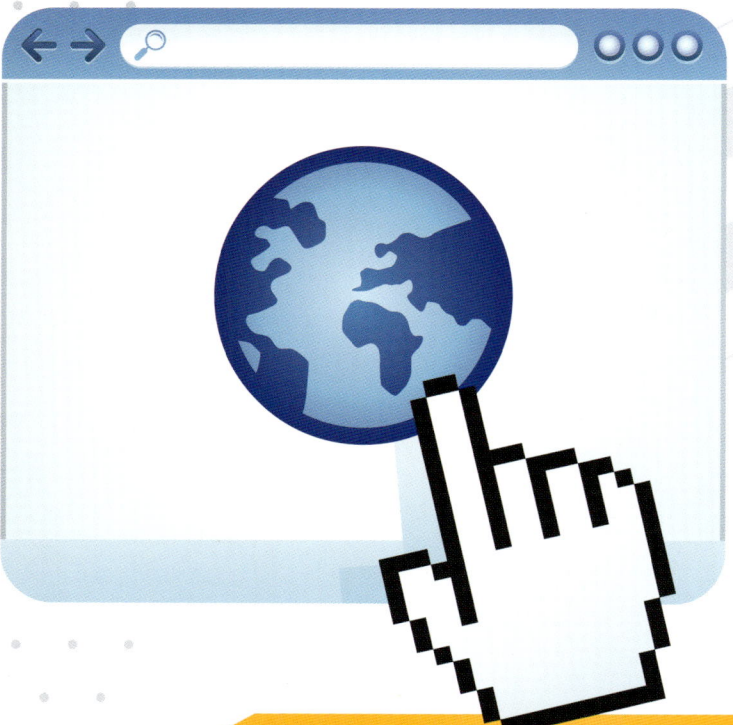

- Internet Explorer
- Chrome
- Safari
- Firefox
- Edge

NETSCAPE NAVIGATOR

The first web browser developed into Netscape Navigator in the 1990s. Student researchers at a university in the USA invented it to make searching the Internet easy for users.

How to Resize a Webpage

ON A DESKTOP OR LAPTOP COMPUTER WITH A KEYBOARD

There are a number of ways to resize a webpage so it is easier to read:

1. Press **CTRL-** or **CTRL+** to make a page smaller or larger.
2. Use the **ZOOM** function located under the settings cog wheel in Internet Explorer or in the drop-down box in the top right-hand corner of Google Chrome.

ON A SMARTPHONE OR TABLET

1. Pinch with two fingers on the screen to make a webpage larger or smaller.

Web Browsers Offer Some or All of These Functions:

1. Scroll bars down the side and at the bottom of the screen so that users can move to anywhere on the webpage

2. Hyperlinks to other webpages

3. The URL or webpage address in the address bar

4. A padlock in the address bar showing the security status of the webpage

5. The title of the webpage at the top of the screen

6. Toolbar icons that allow a user to move to a previous webpage, or to refresh the screen or to stop a webpage loading

7. A 'Home' icon to send the user to the webpage they have set as their own home page

8. The ability to mark webpages as Favourites so they are easy to find next time

9. Security settings that a user can select for themselves

10. Buttons to allow deletion of browsing history

11. Buttons to allow minimising or restoring the whole browser page

Security and Web Browsers

Web browsers offer a choice of security settings. Some of the settings that a user should set when they are using a browser for the first time are:

- Whether to accept cookies
- Whether to allow websites to know your location
- Whether to allow a website to access the computer's camera or microphone
- Whether to show all images
- Whether to block pop-ups
- Whether to allow all automatic downloads

Pop-Ups

Some of these security settings can be difficult to set for people who do not understand the way a browser works. For example, allowing pop-ups can leave your computer vulnerable to receiving constant, annoying advertising. However, some forms that you need to fill in, or safe information that you want to see, also use pop-ups.

Security Software

Internet users should consider adding commercial security software to their computers. These software packages can protect a computer from being infected with viruses and malware via the Internet. Security software also offers notifications that will warn if a website appears to have dangerous links in it.

A firewall is a system designed to prevent unauthorised access to or from a private computer network.

Mmmm! Cookies!
Q: Can I eat them?
A: No. Cookies are little pieces of coding that a webpage uses to determine your browsing habits or preferences.

World Wide Web

The Internet and the World Wide Web are not the same thing. The Internet refers to the millions of connected computers that can exchange information. The World Wide Web refers to the resources that the computers share. These resources include documents, images, videos and sounds. Most people use the word 'Internet' to refer to both the computer networks and the webpage documents.

URLs

URLs, or Uniform Resource Locators, are the way that the Internet finds the particular page a user is searching for. Each of the resources on the World Wide Web has a unique URL. It appears in the address bar at the top of the browser for every page or other resource on the Internet. URLs are also called web addresses.

If you want to share an interesting webpage with someone else, copy the URL from the address bar of the Internet browser, then paste the URL into an email to that person. Because the URL directs a user only to that single page out of the billions in the World Wide Web, the receiver of your email will be able to find and open it quickly.

There are four main parts to a URL, such as this one on the Internet

http://www.redbackpublishing.com/about-us/index.html

http://	www.redbackpublishing.com/	about-us/	Index.html
protocol	domain name	path	file name

parts of a domain name		
www	redbackpublishing	com
World Wide Web	domain name	used for a business website. Governments will use .gov and organisations will use .org

WEBSITE Q & A

Q: What is a website?

A: A website is a collection of webpages linked together under the one domain name and available for searching on the Internet.

Troubleshooting the Internet

9 Troubleshooting Tips

When the Internet will not connect on your computer or device, try these 9 troubleshooting steps:

1. Check all the cables are plugged in properly.

2. Switch the computer, the modem and the router off then on again after a few seconds.

3. Try opening a different website to check if the problem is with one website only.

4. Try using a different computer to check if the problem is with one computer only.

5. If you are using your Internet connection at home, switch off Wi-Fi on your mobile phone or tablet and use its mobile data to check if the Internet works. If it does, this suggests you have a problem with your modem or router.

6. Very high usage of the Internet by other people can slow down the connection speeds for everyone.

7. Run a security check on your computer in case you have a virus.

8. Check that you have not exceeded your ISP data allowance.

9. Error 404 means that the webpage address you entered does not exist. Try going to the website's home page instead and navigate from there to the information you want.

404

Oops...page not found

Who Pays for the Internet?

The existence of the Internet depends on electricity, internationally connected cables and on satellites. This expensive infrastructure needs to be paid for, both by governments and individuals. The Internet is not free. Even when we are using free Wi-Fi, someone has to pay for it.

Internet Service Providers (ISPs)

To connect to the Internet, users need to pay for this service through an ISP, or Internet Service Provider. The amount of data a user can buy is measured in megabytes or gigabytes. People who use the Internet for a lot of downloading may find that they run out of megabytes. In this case, their ISP may either stop providing the Internet service, or slow it down.

Mobile Data Usage

The megabyte allowance on mobile devices and laptops allows users to connect to the Internet wherever they can receive a mobile phone signal.

HERE ARE 6 WAYS TO REDUCE YOUR MOBILE DATA USAGE:

1. Use your home Wi-Fi whenever you are at home. In your Settings, configure your mobile device so it connects automatically as soon as you are within range.

2. Close all apps when not using them. Some apps continually use your data to send messages back and forth.

3. Do not allow apps to look for your location unless you need them to do this when the app is being used. Checking your location uses up data.

4. Disable Bluetooth unless you really need it.

5. Get into the habit of checking your data usage frequently so you know which actions use up the most data.

6. Don't allow your mobile device to automatically download emails. Check your emails manually when you are near free Wi-Fi.

Webpage Structures

Graphic designers try to make webpages look attractive and easy-to-use. There are many different types of layout, but webpages all need a few basic elements to make them really useful.

Address Bar

The address bar appears right at the top of a browser. It shows the Internet address of the page. Look for the padlock symbol at the beginning of the address to check that a webpage is safe to use.

Banner Header

The banner header is an element that spans the top of a webpage. It may contain words and images and is an important design feature to encourage people to look at the rest of the webpage.

Headlines

Just as in a book, headlines on a webpage divide the content into sections.

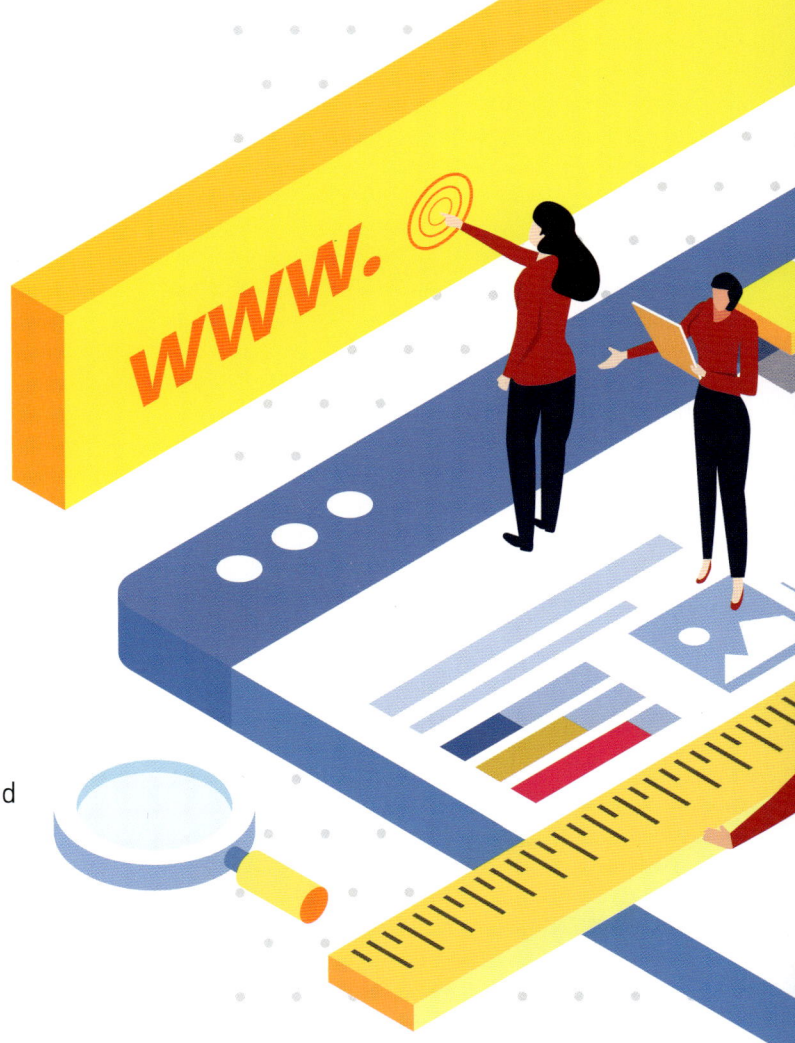

Body Content

The body content is usually the main part of a webpage. It is the section that contains most of the words.

Hyperlink

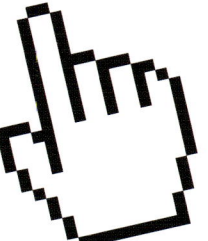

Hyperlinks are links to other webpages. They can be words or images and they usually display differently when a mouse hovers over them. This tells the user that they offer a link to somewhere else. This link may go to another page within the same website, or it could send the user to anywhere on the Internet. When the mouse pointer on the screen turns into a pointing hand, you know there is a hyperlink under the text or image that you are pointing at.

GUI

GUI stands for Graphical User Interface. GUIs are images that link to other pages where there is more information on the topic. Web designers use them instead of words as hyperlinks. As well as making a webpage attractive to look at, GUIs are useful on webpages for children who have not yet learned to read well.

Email Link

Some hyperlinks do not direct the user to another webpage or website. Instead, they open the user's email program.

Images

The Internet would be very dull without images. Some images contain hyperlinks to other webpages. Programmers can add tags to images that describe their content. This assists people with a visual disability who use programs that read out loud the word content on a webpage.

Image tags are also important for SEO. Search engines can read and index this text.

Menu

The menu usually appears either across the top or bottom of a webpage, or in a column down one side. The menu contains links to other webpages within the same website. It is important to design a menu that makes navigation easy for the user.

Login

Login sections on a webpage are where a user enters their user name and password before gaining access to password protected webpages.

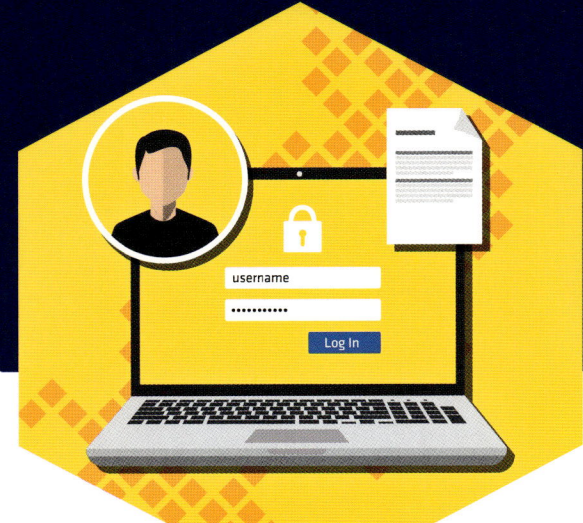

Blog

A blog is an online feature where the blog owner and visitors post content and comments. Having a blog on a website keeps the content updated and allows the website to respond very quickly to changes in the website's subject. A blog is like a diary to which both the creator and other readers can contribute.

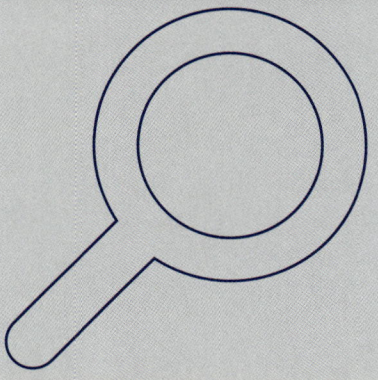

Search

The search box allows a user to locate a word, a product or information if they appear somewhere on the website.

Forms and Surveys

When a website asks the user to fill in an online form, the data travels to the website owner over the Internet. They decide what they will do with this data, so take care before entering any personal detail into an online form. Some websites offer fascinating surveys that ask the computer user to enter details about themselves to find out what sort of character they have, what their future holds, or how clever they are. Some of these sites use the personal details entered by the user to later target them with online advertising.

Home Link

THERE ARE TWO SORTS OF HOME LINKS ON THE INTERNET:

1. Within a website, the home link is a button, image or text that hyperlinks to the home page of the website. The home page is the page that a web browser looks for when it is searching for a website. The home page link is usually located in the top left corner of the webpage.

2. On a web browser, such as Google, the home link at the top of the browser window takes the user to whichever page they have set up as their Internet home page.

HTTP

Hypertext Transfer Protocol, or HTTP, is the standard method used on the Internet to transfer webpages. A web address that starts with 'http' is announcing to the web server that the user's computer wants to receive a webpage constructed using HTTP. People who create webpages do this using HTTP, which is a bit like coding, although HTTP is not really a coding language. Webpage creation software, such as Adobe Dreamweaver, allows a webpage designer to use HTTP codes if they know them, or they can use the WYSIWYG function, which is more like using an ordinary text editor.

 https://

Look for HTTPS in the address bar to ensure you are visiting a secure website.

WYSIWYG

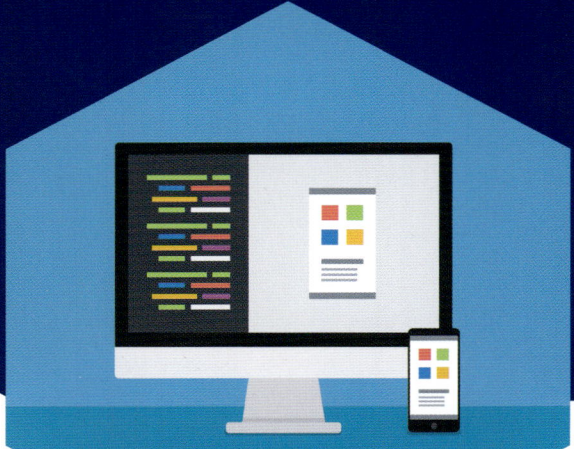

WYSIWYG, or What You See Is What You Get, is a function offered in some software programs which allows the user to create content using normal text, without having to understand much coding. WYSIWYG software looks like a text editor program to the user, but it creates the content in specialised computer languages that the user does not see on the screen. Some HTTP software offers WYSIWYG functions for users who want to create webpages for the Internet.

Lorem Ipsum

These are the first two words in a passage of Latin text that website designers use as a placeholder. The words have no connection with the website content. Their purpose is to fill a space so that a designer can see whether the layout looks artistically pleasing.

Metadata

Metadata on webpages is data about data. On a webpage, the metadata includes the title of the page that appears at the top of the browser, and keywords added to the webpage code as meta tags, which the user cannot normally see. The purpose of webpage metadata is to make the webpages more visible to search engines. Users are then more likely to see the webpage listed higher when they do a browser search.

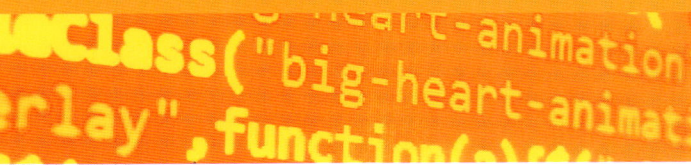

Internet Structures

IP Addresses

IP stands for Internet Protocol. An IP address is a string of numbers that identifies every device that can connect to the Internet. Every Internet connected mobile phone, computer, printer or smart TV has its own IP address. If all these devices connect to the Internet through a router, then the router uses only its own IP address when it makes an online connection.

Web Servers and Clients

Web servers are computers that provide webpages when requested to by clients. Clients are the browsers on the users' computers.

Apps

An app is software that is downloaded, usually to a mobile device. Apps differ from websites by having their code located on the user's device, rather than on a web server. Using apps often reduces the megabyte usage for downloads, since much of the content is already on the user's own mobile device. Both apps and websites connect via the Internet to servers, and they both use the mobile device's data allowance.

WEB SERVERS

Connecting the Internet

Dial-Up

When the general public first started connecting to the Internet in the 1990s, they often used a dial-up service. This needed a telephone line. A computer and the telephone could not be used at the same time on the same line.

Broadband

Computers on the Internet can interact using a broadband connection. The term 'broadband' means that the physical connection can carry a large amount of data.

Satellite Broadband

In remote areas, people can access the Internet using signals from a satellite orbiting the Earth. The signal is captured by a satellite dish and then eventually conveyed to the network of the Internet Service Provider that the user has chosen.

Fake News and Information

10 TIPS
for Spotting Fake News & Information on the Internet

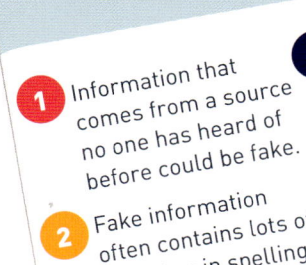

1 Information that comes from a source no one has heard of before could be fake.

2 Fake information often contains lots of mistakes in spelling and grammar.

3 Fake news tends to make sensational and outrageous claims about famous people.

4 Trusted news reports include the name of the journalist and the date of the post.

5 Fake news often includes old photographs from events that are not connected with the current report.

6 Fake information sites may contain links and downloads that will send viruses and malware to a user's computer.

7 Fake information sites may try to persuade a user to hand over personal information which is then used for annoying advertising or even for criminal purposes.

8 Fake news uses almost unbelievable headlines to gain a reader's attention. The content may actually have little connection with the meaning of the headline.

9 If no other reliable Internet source is reporting the same information, this suggests that the original report may be fake.

10 Fake information does not offer any proof for its claims.

FAKE NEWS

DOWNLOAD A COPY OF THIS POSTER TO USE AT HOME OR AT SCHOOL

- Go to www.redbackpublishing.com
- Find the entry for this book and click on the link for the Fake News poster.

Social Media

Social media, such as Facebook, Instagram, Twitter, Pinterest, WhatsApp and Snapshot all use the Internet to send messages back and forth.

WHO'S ONLINE?

The first internationally popular social media service was MySpace in the early 2000s. Many users were not familiar with the dangers of social media, and became victims of online stalkers and trolls. This unfortunate trend is still continuing.

BE SAFE ONLINE

People who use social media need to be aware of safe practices. These include never providing personal information to strangers, and not believing everything that people say online.

STAYING CONNECTED

Users of all ages find social media interesting and even vital to their lifestyles. Children use it to connect with friends, politicians use it to get their message out to voters, businesses use it to promote their goods and services, and celebrities use it to connect with their fans.

AGE LIMITS

All social media websites and apps have age limits for users. This is to discourage children from using their services without supervision.

Online Shopping

Online shopping using the Internet is a major force in the world's retail industries. Shops need an Internet presence to appeal to the shoppers who do not want to have to travel to buy what they want or need.

The increase in the usage of online shopping has resulted in a corresponding increase in the use of post and couriers for the delivery of all the things people have bought. Whether the delivery is in the same suburb or across the world, many parcel delivery services have benefited from the widespread use of the Internet for shopping.

Online shopping is not just for people who love to shop. Disabled or sick people who cannot travel easily use online shopping to buy what they need.

IN-STORE OR ONLINE?

'BRICKS & MORTAR' STORES

- Shopping can be a fun, social experience
- Easy to check quality of goods
- Easy to check if clothes fit
- Can take shopping home with you

ONLINE STORES

- Convenient
- No need to travel
- Easy to compare prices
- Have to wait for delivery

Emails

Emails need the Internet. They have overtaken letter sending as a method of communicating in writing.

Email Clients

Popular email software includes Microsoft Outlook, Hotmail, Yahoo! and Gmail. These are called email clients.

Email Servers

Email servers hold lists of all the email addresses that they manage. They use these lists to make sure emails they receive are made available to the correct destinations.

Bouncebacks

Bouncebacks happen when an email address has an error in it. Because of this error, the email server does not recognise the email address and rejects the request to receive the email.

Writing an Email

When letters were the main way that people wrote to each other, there were rules about how to lay them out and how to select special words to use in certain parts of the letter, such as the beginning and end. Emails are quicker to write and send, but they still have rules about the way to use them.

EMAIL ETIQUETTE

- Using all capitals suggests that you are shouting
- Avoid using emojis in a letter to a business
- Sign the email
- Use a simple and descriptive Subject line
- People tend to not read long emails
- Keep unusual punctuation to a minimum
- Think twice before sending an email if you are feeling angry or upset

Email Security

Cyber criminals and bullies use emails to upset people and damage their computers with viruses and malware. All email users, both children and grown-ups, should be aware of online security so they can protect themselves and their computers.

Security Software

Computers should all have security software installed on them to guard against infection by viruses that come with emails. Emails with harmful attachments may look innocent, but they will start doing their damage as soon as the user clicks on an infectious link.

Passwords

Email passwords should be 'strong'. A strong password is one which is difficult to guess and which contains a mixture of words, numbers and symbols.

Scams

Scams can be in the form of emails from people who pretend to offer amazing deals, large discounts on goods, tickets to events, and many other bogus goods and services. If an offer is not from a well-known source and is promising something that seems too good to be true, do not open the email.

Phishing

Phishing emails attempt to persuade the user to submit personal details in exchange for free goods, to join a group, or perhaps to fill out a survey. The people sending phishing emails may use the information they have obtained to undertake criminal activities.

Spam

Spam is unwanted email advertising. It may flood a user's inbox and be very annoying.

Grooming

When an adult stranger pretends to build a friendship with a child by email or social media, and the adult has criminal intentions, this is called grooming. Groomers may send the child photos of someone else while claiming that it is a selfie.

Replying to Strangers

Children who receive emails from strangers should never open them or reply to them.

Attachments

Viruses can arrive at your computer as an email attachment. Avoid opening attachments from email addresses you do not recognise.

Junk File

To stop receiving unwanted emails, mark them as Junk. This will send any future emails from the same source to the Junk folder. Browse the Junk folder regularly without opening any of the emails, just in case an email you do want has gone there by mistake.

Delete

Delete suspicious emails from the Deleted folder. This will stop you from accidentally clicking on a dangerous link in the future. Just as you have to put out the garbage at home to be taken away, you also need to keep your email folders clean by deleting unwanted content.

Tell a Trusted Adult

If you think your computer may have a virus, if a stranger keeps contacting you, or if you are being bullied by email, tell a trusted adult right away. The longer you keep it a secret, the worse the situation could become.

Logging Off at the Library

When using a public computer at a library or at school, always log off when you are finished looking at your emails. This will stop anyone else from being able to access your emails.

Is It Real?

There are a number of warning signs that suggest an email you have received could be dangerous:

- The email claims to be official but it contains spelling and grammar mistakes
- The email address looks unusual
- The email asks for your passwords
- The email says you owe money when you know that is not true
- The layout looks unprofessional

Research Before the Internet Existed

The Internet has become the favourite source for people around the world who need information. Whether they want to self-diagnose an illness, find a location or a simple recipe, or research a serious scientific project, the Internet is everyone's first choice.

Libraries

The Internet for public use has only been around since the 1990s. Before that, books were the main source of information. Public libraries developed from the 1930s to allow people who could not afford to buy a book on every subject to still be able to find out any information they needed. The role of Reference Librarians was to help people find what they wanted amongst the millions of books published.

Private Book Collections

People who could afford to buy many books kept their own private libraries of non-fiction books so they would have immediate access to information, without having to go out to a library to find it. Some families provided expensive sets of encyclopedias at home for their children.

News Services

Today we can search the Internet for a news report from a year ago. Before the Internet, services existed which summarised the news and sold these summaries as a weekly, indexed report on paper.

Government Information

People who wanted information about government activities and services needed to make telephone calls or visit a library to see if there was a publication that explained what they wanted to know. Statistical information was published in regular reports on paper that researchers could use in a public library.

Tech Terms for Kids

computer settings	set of computer instructions
computer virus	damaging code that infects a computer
configure	set up in a special way
cookie	code that a website places on a user's computer
copyright	ownership of a creative work
Dark Web	encrypted section of the Internet
dial-up	accessing the Internet by dialling the phone number of the ISP
domain name	part of a web address
encrypt	make unreadable by using a secret code
fake news	news containing lies
firewall	used to secure a computer or network and block unauthorised access
GUI	Graphical User Interface
HTTP	Hypertext Transfer Protocol
hyperlink	link to another webpage
IP address	numbers that make up an Internet Protocol address
ISP	Internet Service Provider
keyword	word that has special impact in a search
malware	malicious software
metadata	data about other data
online scam	online activity to obtain money or other benefits illegally
phish	attempt to get personal details of a person online
pop-up	box that pops up over the top of a webpage
protocol	set of instructions for doing something
search engine	software to search the Internet
selfie	photograph taken of oneself
SEO	Search Engine Optimisation
software algorithm	computer code for completing a process
spam	unwanted email advertising
troll	person who makes harmful comments about others online
URL	Uniform Resource Locator
web browser	program that allows connection to the Internet
WWW	World Wide Web
WYSIWYG	What You See Is What You Get

index